The Cheyenne

by Allison Lassieur

Consultant:
Gordon Yellowman
Cultural Liaison
Southern Cheyenne and Arapaho Tribes of Oklahoma

Bridgestone Books
an imprint of Capstone Press
Mankato, Minnesota

Bridgestone Books are published by Capstone Press
151 Good Counsel Drive, P.O. Box 669, Mankato, Minnesota 56002
http://www.capstone-press.com

Library of Congress Cataloging-in-Publication Data
Lassieur, Allison.
    The Cheyenne/by Allison Lassieur.
      p. cm.—(Native peoples)
    Includes bibliographical references and index.
    ISBN 0-7368-0831-0
    1. Cheyenne Indians—History—Juvenile literature. 2. Cheyenne Indians—Social life
and customs—Juvenile literature. [1. Cheyenne Indians. 2. Indians of North America—
Great Plains.] I. Title. II. Series.
E99.C53 C54 2001
973'.04973—dc21
                                                                            00-009929

Summary: An overview of the past and present lives of the Cheyenne including their
   history, food and clothing, homes and family life, religion, and government.

Editorial Credits
Rebecca Glaser, editor; Karen Risch, product planning editor; Timothy Halldin, cover
   designer; Heather Kindseth, production designer; Linda Clavel, illustrator; Heidi Schoof,
   photo researcher

Photo Credits
Corbis, 20
Corel Corporation, 18
Gordon Yellowman, 14
Historic Fort Reno Visitor's Center, cover, 10
Index Stock Imagery/Allen Russell, 8, 12
Photo Network, 16
Stock Montage, 6

1 2 3 4 5 6 06 05 04 03 02 01

Table of Contents

Map. 4
Fast Facts 5

Cheyenne History .7
The Cheyenne People 9
Homes, Food, and Clothing 11
The Cheyenne Family 13
Cheyenne Religion 15
Sweet Medicine 17
The Origin of the Buffalo 19
Cheyenne Government 21

Hands On: Make a Namshim Drum 22
Words to Know 23
Read More 23
Useful Addresses. 24
Internet Sites 24
Index. 24

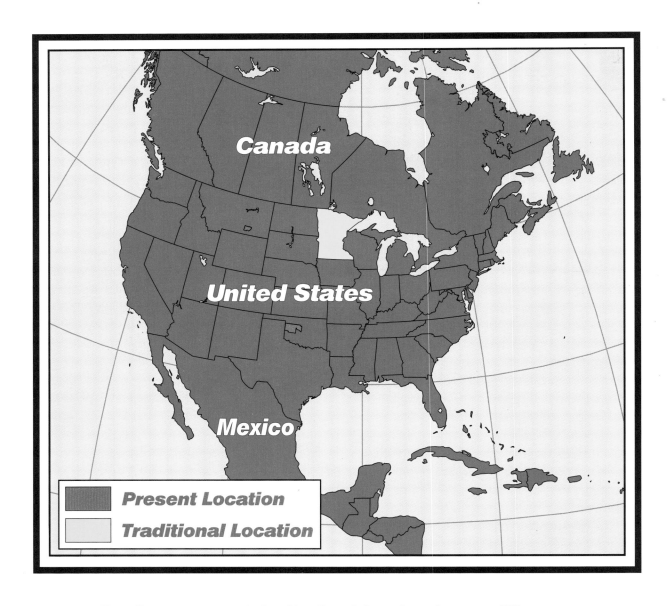

**The Cheyenne originally lived in what is now Minnesota.
Today, most Cheyenne live in Montana and Oklahoma.**

Fast Facts

Two groups of Cheyenne live in the United States today. The Northern Cheyenne live on a reservation in Lame Deer, Montana. The Southern Cheyenne live in western Oklahoma. Today the Cheyenne live like other North Americans. These facts describe past Cheyenne traditions.

Homes: The earliest Cheyenne lived in earth lodges made of wood and sod. They later built tepees from wood poles and buffalo hides.

Food: Long ago, the Cheyenne grew corn, beans, and squash on farms. They later gave up farming and began to hunt buffalo. Men fished with willow nets. Women gathered berries, roots, and seeds.

Clothing: In warm weather, men wore deerskin breechcloths around their waists. Women wore deerskin dresses. Everyday clothing was simple. Cheyenne decorated clothing for special ceremonies with beads, bells, and fringe.

Language: The Cheyenne language is an Algonquian language. People who speak one Algonquian language usually can understand other Algonquian languages.

The Battle of Little Bighorn

One of the most famous battles between American Indians and the U.S. Army is the Battle of Little Bighorn. In June 1876, the Sioux joined the Cheyenne to fight U.S. General George Custer and his troops. The Indians defeated Custer's troops and killed more than 200 U.S. soldiers.

Cheyenne History

Long ago, the Cheyenne were farmers in what is now Minnesota. European explorers brought horses to North America. The Cheyenne adapted the horse into their way of life. They stopped farming and traveled across the Great Plains to hunt buffalo.

In the early 1800s, the Cheyenne split into two groups. The Northern Cheyenne stayed on the plains to hunt buffalo. The Southern Cheyenne moved to Colorado.

A few years later, European settlers began to take Northern Cheyenne lands. The Cheyenne fought back. They were at war with the U.S. Army for many years. The Cheyenne had several victories. But in the end, the U.S. Army won.

The U.S. government forced the Southern Cheyenne to move to Oklahoma. The Northern Cheyenne were put on a reservation in Montana.

The Cheyenne People

The Cheyenne call themselves Tsisiststas. This word means "the people" or "beautiful." The name Cheyenne probably came from the Sioux word shahiyena. It means "people of different speech."

The Cheyenne are trying to keep their language alive. Many Northern Cheyenne children learn the Cheyenne language in school on the reservation. Other children learn it from their parents and grandparents. Each child receives both an English name and a Cheyenne name. In public, people use their English names. With family and friends, most people use their Cheyenne names.

Today, the Cheyenne live in Montana or Oklahoma. Some Cheyenne work for the tribe as firefighters or security guards. Many Cheyenne work for the casino owned by the tribe.

The Cheyenne respect the traditions, beliefs, and culture of their ancestors. The Cheyenne still follow some of the old ways.

The Cheyenne celebrate their traditions at powwows.

Homes, Food, and Clothing

The farming Cheyenne built earth lodges by covering wooden poles with earth and sod. On the plains, the Cheyenne built tepees. The Cheyenne arranged poles in a cone shape and covered them with buffalo hides. Tepees were easy to move.

As farmers, the Cheyenne grew corn, beans, and squash. Women took care of gardens. Men hunted animals such as deer, squirrels, and rabbits. Later, the Cheyenne used buffalo for food, clothing, and homes. Women also gathered berries and roots such as turnips from the plains.

In the past, the Cheyenne made clothes from animal skins. For special occasions, they decorated their clothing with brightly colored beads. They wore buffalo robes to keep warm in winter. Later, the Cheyenne made clothes from cloth. Today, the Cheyenne wear clothes like those of other North Americans.

The Cheyenne decorated their tepees with painted designs.

The Cheyenne Family

In the past, Cheyenne women were caretakers. They took care of the gardens and the children. Cheyenne men were braves. They hunted and fought in battles.

Cheyenne children began to learn traditional roles while they were young. Many Cheyenne children had "play camps." They made small play tepees. They pretended that their dogs were horses. Boys hunted and girls made food. This way, they practiced doing adult jobs.

A Cheyenne man had to ask permission from a woman's family to marry her. When both families agreed on the marriage, they held a ceremony. The families exchanged gifts and had a feast. The man and woman then went to live in a tepee near the woman's mother.

Family is important to the Cheyenne. The Cheyenne always take care of children in the tribe. If something happens to a child's parents, another family adopts the child.

Cheyenne families often take part in powwows.

The Cheyenne gathered each spring for the Sun Dance. The Cheyenne built a circular lodge from tree poles for the ceremony. They still hold the Sun Dance today.

Cheyenne Religion

The Cheyenne believe that powerful spirits live in the world. These spirits exist in the four directions—north, south, east, and west. The number four is special to Cheyenne beliefs.

In the past, the Cheyenne held ceremonies to pray to the spirits. They held the Sun Dance ceremony to help renew the earth for the coming year. Each spring, all the Cheyenne came together. They built a special lodge for the ceremony and sang sacred songs. The ceremony lasted four days. The Cheyenne gave thanks to the spirits and asked for protection from sickness or danger.

The Cheyenne still follow traditional beliefs today. They hold the Sun Dance each summer.

Sweet Medicine

Sweet Medicine was a Cheyenne prophet who lived very long ago. The Great Spirit gave Sweet Medicine instruction on the Cheyenne way of life. Sweet Medicine received a special bundle from the Great Spirit at the sacred mountain Bear Butte.

Today, the Southern Cheyenne keep the special bundle in Oklahoma. The Bundle Keeper is an important member of the tribe.

The spirits made many predictions about the Cheyenne's future through Sweet Medicine's teachings. His teachings still live on today.

Five societies still are maintained by traditional leaders. These societies follow the teachings of Sweet Medicine. They are the Elk Society, Bowstring Society, Kit Fox Society, Dog Soldiers, and the Council of Forty-Four.

Sweet Medicine received a special bundle at Bear Butte near present-day Sturgis, South Dakota.

The Origin of the Buffalo

This story tells how the buffalo came to the Cheyenne. Long ago, the Cheyenne were hungry. The chief asked three braves to look for food in a nearby cave. The braves held hands and jumped into the dark cave opening.

They saw a door and knocked. An old grandmother answered. "What do you want?" she asked. "The people are hungry," the braves said. The braves went through the doorway. The grandmother pointed to a window. The braves looked out. They saw a wide prairie with great herds of buffalo.

The grandmother gave each brave a bowl of buffalo meat. The bowls stayed full as they ate. "Take these magic bowls to your people," the grandmother said. "Soon I will send live buffalo."

The braves brought the bowls to their people. Everyone ate buffalo meat. The next day, buffalo appeared near the village. The Cheyenne thanked the grandmother and the spirits for the buffalo.

The Cheyenne used buffalo for food, clothing, and shelter.

Cheyenne Government

Long ago, the Cheyenne were governed by the Council of Forty-Four. Members of this council became peace chiefs. Peace chiefs stayed in office for 10 years. Peace chiefs set an example for the tribe. The council made decisions based on opinions of the tribe.

Today, the Cheyenne government has two parts. The business committee is responsible for the tribe's money. The Southern Cheyenne and Arapaho tribes are united. Four Cheyenne and four Arapaho make up the business committee. The Cheyenne also have a tribal council. Every Cheyenne over the age of 18 is a member. The tribal council meets once each year. They talk about ways to help the tribe.

The Cheyenne still have the Council of Forty-Four. Men earn the right to be a council chief by living a good, honest life. The council does not make rules or decisions. Instead, the chiefs give advice and speak on issues that concern the tribe.

Chief Dull Knife was a famous chief of the Northern Cheyenne. Dull Knife Memorial College in Lame Deer, Montana, is named for him.

Hands On: Make a Namshim Drum

Drums are an important part of many Cheyenne ceremonies. The word namshim means "grandfather." The Cheyenne respect their drums as though they are part of the family. You can make a namshim drum.

What You Need

Old newspapers
Large coffee can
Paints and paint brush
Kitchen garbage bag

Large and small rubber bands
New, unsharpened pencils
Scraps of cloth

What You Do

1. Spread old newspapers over your work area to protect it.
2. Paint the coffee can white. When the white paint is dry, paint colorful designs on the can. Let the paint dry.
3. Cut a square of plastic from the kitchen garbage bag that is 12 inches by 12 inches (30 centimeters by 30 centimeters).
4. Stretch the plastic over the open end of the coffee can. Use a large rubber band to hold the plastic in place. Make sure the plastic is stretched tight.
5. Wrap the scraps of cloth around one end of a pencil to make a drum beater. Use a small rubber band to hold the cloth in place. Make two drum beaters.

In Cheyenne tradition, only men are allowed to play drums. Women sing songs while the men play.

Words to Know

ancestor (AN-sess-tur)—a member of one's family who lived a long time ago, such as a great-grandparent

breechcloth (BREECH-kloth)—a piece of deerskin clothing that hangs from the waist and passes between the legs

casino (kuh-SEE-noh)—a place where adults bet money on the outcome of games

ceremony (SER-eh-moh-nee)—formal actions, words, and often music that honor a person, event, or a higher being

religion (ri-LIJ-uhn)—a set of spiritual beliefs people follow

reservation (res-er-VAY-shun)—land owned and controlled by American Indians

sacred (SAY-krid)—very important and deserving great respect; sacred objects are related to a religion.

tepee (TEE-pee)—a cone-shaped tent made of animal skins

tradition (truh-DISH-uhn)—a custom, idea, or belief that is passed on to younger people by older relatives

Read More

Bonvillain, Nancy. *The Cheyennes: People of the Plains.* Native Americans. Brookfield, Conn.: Millbrook Press, 1996.

Meli, Franco. *A Day with a Cheyenne.* Minneapolis: Runestone Press, 1999.

Sneve, Virginia Driving Hawk. *The Cheyennes.* A First Americans Book. New York: Holiday House, 1996.

Useful Addresses

Northern Cheyenne Tribal Council
P.O. Box 128
Lame Deer, MT 59043

Southern Cheyenne and Arapaho Tribes
P.O. Box 38
Concho, OK 73022

Internet Sites

Cheyenne
http://www.geocities.com/Athens/Oracle/5863/cheyenne.html
Cheyenne and Arapaho Tribes of Oklahoma
http://www.cheyenne-arapaho.org/home.htm
Northern Cheyenne Tribe
http://www.cheyennetour.com/nctribe.html

Index

Bear Butte, 17
buffalo, 7, 11, 19
casino, 9
Council of Forty-Four, 17, 21
earth lodges, 11
family, 9, 13
gardens, 11, 13
Great Plains, 7

language, 9
Northern Cheyenne, 7, 9
Southern Cheyenne, 7, 17
Sun Dance, 15
Sweet Medicine, 17
tepee, 11, 13
traditional roles, 13
Tsisiststas, 9